Captain Sparky

and the

Pool Pirates

T. E. ANTONINO

T. E. Antonino

Captain Sparky and the Pool Pirates

Copyright © 2023 T. E. Antonino

Acknowledgements

I thank Hannah Dargan, my editor.

She is an exceptional editor, and I value all of her creative suggestions.

This is the sixth book she has edited for me.

Books by T. E. Antonino

ShBeep the Unique Sheep

Fritz Fombie Have No Fear

Fritz Fombie and the Frightful Feats of Courage

Front Cover artwork

The front cover and inside illustrations were hand drawn by the author. The coloring of the front cover was done in colored pencil by Roberta Antonino and the author. Alex Cracchiolo did finishing touches with a graphic design program. I thank both of them for their artistic suggestions.

The wind whirls
The sea swirls
The night chills
I stood my ground
The bowing brave
The fleeing night
The coming light
I am Captain Sparky

Chapter 1

The English Homework

I was like every other fourth-grade kid until the day I became a pirate. Let me change that to the day I became a pirate captain. What? You don't think a little girl is tough enough to become a pirate captain? Well, you better watch out because I'm as tough as snails, and I'll stand up to any chilly williwaw the sea can whip up.

"Sparky, it's time to stop playing in the pool. We need to go," my mom said as she sat up in the pool deck sun chair. "Wait one minute! What just poked its head out of your swimsuit pocket?"

"It was a fly," I said.

"A fly my foot. You brought Morris, your pet turtle, to the pool with you again, didn't you?"

"I need Morris to teach me how to swim or float or both," I said.

"I'm not taking you to the pool anymore if you keep sneaking Morris in with you."

"Fine, I'll just have to splash around in the baby pool for the rest of my life while the other kids get to swim in the big pool."

"Sparky, I told you not to worry about being able to swim yet. Only fish, pirates, or a hippopotamus need to worry about being able to swim. And I'm serious about that turtle. I don't want you bringing him into the pool with you anymore. Now we should be going."

"Can't I just splash around in the pool for a little bit longer, please?"

"Ok, just a little longer, then we're headed home," Mom said. "And you need to be trying to come up with a story for your English class tomorrow. The English homework in your backpack said you can use a dictionary to put fun words into your story."

"What story?" I mumbled to myself as I stomped the water with my red rubber rain boots. I wore rubber rain boots because I didn't like getting my feet wet, even in the baby pool.

"We're having turkey for dinner," Mom said. "You could write a story about a turkey."

"I will never, ever write a story about a turkey," I said. "There's nothing left to write about anyway. Every story that can be written has been written.

We'll have to wait for someone to make up more words before I can write a story."

"I'm not buying that for one minute," Mom said. "How about writing a story about a crab or a duck? They like water as much as you do."

"I'm not writing a story about a crab or a duck!" I said. "Crabs are mean, and all ducks do is go quack, quack."

"When we get home, I want to see you making more than squid squiggles with your pencil. I want to see a story," Mom said. "Now, I'm going to the pool locker room to change, then we have to leave."

Coming up with a story was hopeless, so I reached into my swimsuit pocket and pulled out Morris my pet turtle. I rubbed Morris's head like a lucky charm, but still no story. As I put Morris back into my swimsuit pocket, I found a penny. Could this be a wishing well penny? I made a wish. Then I patted my head and rubbed my belly at the same time, but still no story.

I plopped down in the water, and that's when my luck changed. The pool water bubbled and rumbled. The north wind blew strong. A monsoon, a cloudburst, and a gullywasher hit all at once.

Deep End
2 Feet

Chapter 2
Gobble, Bobble, and Wobble

Out of the pool drain, three pirates popped out.

"Hello, my name's Gobble, and I'm a pirate."

"I can see you're a pirate. My name is Sparky. I like your stocking hat with that ball on top."

"Hello, my name is Bobble, and I'm a pirate."

"I can see you're a pirate, too. My name is Sparky. I like your mop top of red hair. Red hair is super cool."

"Hello, I'm Captain Wobble, and I'm a pirate."

"I can see you're also a pirate. My name is Sparky. I like the feather in your tricorn hat. It's pretty snazzy."

"We could all hear the watery fuss you're making from way down below in the water pipes," Captain Wobble said.

"A very big watery fuss," Gobble said.

"The fussiest of watery fusses," Bobble said. "If you made any more of a ruckus, you would sink the pool."

"Now that does sound like real fun!" I said.

"Only a pirate or a sea hippopotamus can cause a watery hoo-ha like you're doing," Bobble said.

"I'm not a hippopotamus. If I were a hippopotamus, I would live in water. Well, I'm in a pool filled with water, but I don't live in the pool. I live in a house. What I'm trying to say is I'm a girl, and I'm nothing at all like a hippopotamus."

"That means you must be a pirate, and you're in our waters, where you shouldn't be," Captain Wobble growled.

"We should flush you down the pool drain," Bobble said.

"Down the pipes and out to the sea you'll go," Gobble said.

"We won't even close our eyes when a sea hippopotamus swallows you whole," Captain Wobble said.

"That's not a very nice thing to say," I said. "You should watch your words or people will think you're mean."

Bobble, Gobble, and Captain Wobble's heads sunk down low at the same time.

"Nobody likes us," Wobble said.

"People look at us and run away," Bobble said.

"No one thinks pirates can be nice," Captain Wobble said. "We should just go back to our pirate ship in the pool pipes below and stay there forever."

"How about we make a deal," I said. "What if I teach you to be nice, and you can teach me to be a pirate?"

"Now that's something to think about for sure," Bobble said.

"That might just work," Gobble said.

"Sparky, my pirate crew and I would like to talk this deal of yours over," Captain Wobble said.

"Sure, go ahead," I said as I picked up the pool beach ball and tossed it up and down.

The pirates swam over to the far side of the baby pool.

"I think she'll make a fine pirate," Captain Wobble whispered.

"Very fine pirate," Gobble whispered.

"The best of pirates," Bobble whispered.

"If Sparky can teach us to be nice, maybe people would like us," Captain Wobble said.

"Some say it's helpless for a pirate to try and be nice," Gobble said.

"Hopefully that's not true," Bobble said.

"There's more hope in hopeful, than help in helpless," Captain Wobble said. "I say we make the deal."

The three pirates swam back over to me.

"All three of us pirates think you would make a fine pirate," Captain Wobble said.

"It's a deal then," I said. "I'll teach you to be nice and you can teach me to be a pirate."

"Let's shake boots on it," Captain Wobble said.

"Don't you mean shake hands?" I asked.

"Pirates shake boots, not hands," Captain Wobble said.

"Why?" I asked.

"If you shake hands with a pirate, it leaves the pirate's other hand free to swipe gold coins out of your pockets," Bobble said.

"That makes sense. I mean it doesn't make sense, but if you're a pirate, I'm sure it makes sense."

All three pirates shook a boot in the air. I lifted one of my red rubber boots and shook it in the air, too.

The deal was made. Gobble, Bobble, and Captain Wobble would teach me to be a pirate, and I would teach the pirates to be nice.

Chapter 3

Share Your Socks

"Tell me more about pirates," I said. "Do pirates have fun?"

"Pirates always have fun," Gobble said. "Unless we sneeze out a rotten tooth."

"I don't have any rotten teeth, but I do have a loose baby tooth. It would be nice if I could sneeze it out. Do pirates mind their manners?"

"Yes," Bobble said. "We blow our noses once a year or when we run out of glue to fix a loose board on the pirate ship deck."

"I'll be thinking about that one for a while. Do pirates put up a fuss when it's bedtime?"

"Never," Captain Wobble said. "Every morning, when the sun comes up, we go right to bed."

"This pirate stuff does sound like a party. I can see that pirates are the crackerjacks of the seven seas."

"You're sure you can teach all of us pirates to be nice?" Captain Wobble asked. "A pirate's heart is as crusty as a copper coin; it won't be easy."

"It'll be a piece of cake. Trust me, you'll be so nice that you'll be sharing each other's socks in no time at all."

Bobble took off a boot and sock. "Gobble, I want to share my sock with you."

"Thank you," Gobble said as he took the sock out of Bobble's hand.

"Gobble, aren't you going to share a sock with me?" Bobble asked. "I just shared my sock with you."

"Nope," Gobble said. "I haven't washed the sock on my right foot in three years. This gives me the chance to give my right sock a good scrubbing and still keep both feet toasty warm."

"Gobble, give me one of your socks right now!" Bobble said.

"I don't think so, but you have a nice rest of your day," Gobble said.

"That's it!" Bobble said. "Gobble, give me back my sock or it's off the end of the plank and into the mouth of a sea hippopotamus for you."

"This is going to be good," Captain Wobble said. "Let's see who ends up in a sea hippopotamus's belly."

"Hold on you two!" I said. "Getting mad over a sock isn't a nice thing to do."

Bobble jumped on Gobble's back. "I want my sock back right now or a sea hippopotamus will have a full belly!"

"Stop it!!!" I said as I threw my hands in the air. "Time out!"

Bobble and Gobble stopped wrestling.

"Nobody is ending up in a sea hippopotamus's belly!" I said.

"Things were just getting fun," Captain Wobble said.

"I wouldn't call ending up in a sea hippopotamus's belly fun. Gobble and Bobble, you two pirates should be ashamed of yourselves."

"But I shared my sock with Gobble, and he didn't share one of his socks with me," Bobble said.

"Bobble, it was nice of you to give your sock to Gobble," I said. "But when you do something nice for someone, you shouldn't ask for anything in return."

"But I have two feet and only one sock," Bobble said.

"I'm going to fix that right now," I said. "Gobble, I want you to think of something nice you could do."

"Going for a long walk on the beach would be nice," Gobble said.

"That's true that would be nice," I said. "But what nice thing could you do for Bobble since he's so upset?"

"I could share one of my socks with Bobble, like he shared his sock with me."

"Now that would be nice," I said.

Gobble took off his right boot and sock, then handed his sock to Bobble.

Bobble grabbed the sock out of Gobble's hand. "Thank you very much."

"That was very nice of both you pirates to share a sock with each other," I said. "Now as for you, Captain Wobble, wanting someone to end up in a sea hippopotamus's belly isn't a nice thing to want, so what should you say?"

"Sorry, Bobble, sorry, Gobble. Wanting someone to end up in a sea hippopotamus's belly isn't nice."

"That's much better. Now how do each of you pirates feel right now?"

"I feel peachy," Bobble said.

"I feel all chummy inside," Gobble said.

"I feel dandy," Captain Wobble said. "I've never felt dandy before."

"That's what being nice does. It brings out the sunshine. Now it's time for me to say goodbye. I have a story to write!"

I tossed the pool beach ball in the air and ran into the pool locker room. I started jumping up and down.

"Now what's up?" Mom asked as she tied her shoes. "You're acting nuttier than a water bug and bedbug dancing the tango on a hot sandy beach."

"There are pirates and socks and tumbling and wrestling and a sea hippopotamus and walking the plank and Wobble, Gobble, and Bobble and...!!!"

"Try and be calm, my child. Speak slowly and clearly so I can understand you."

I shook my arms and legs like a rain-soaked puppy. "I'm calm now."

"Wonderful," Mom said. "So now tell me why you're so excited."

"A story blew in with the wind," I said.

"You're telling me that you came up with a story for English class tomorrow?" Mom asked.

"Yes," I said.

"That's amazing!" Mom said. She grabbed my hand and started running out of the locker room with me. "Let's get you home while this story is still fresh in that bubble bean of yours."

Lickety split and just like that I was in my room, seated at my desk. The north wind blew strong again as I picked up my pencil. I opened my notebook and dictionary. I wrote and wrote some more about the pirates in the pool. That evening I went to bed thinking nice thoughts about pirates. Nice pirates, who would have thought?

Chapter 4

Sparky Becomes a Pirate

My eyes popped open early in the morning. I jumped out of bed and landed on my bedroom floor with a bellyflop. "I have a story to finish writing before my English class, by golly."

I sat at my desk and opened my notebook and dictionary. I turned to a brand new, blank page. I put my pencil on the page, but nothing happened. That's odd. I twirled my pencil and put it on the page again, but nothing happened. I stared at the blank page for ten minutes, but it just stared back.

I sang out, "Pirates, pirates wherever you are, show yourselves. If you don't, I'll be toast without the jelly." There wasn't even a single peep of a pool pirate to be found. I think they call this writer's bark. That's when you have a lot to bark about, but nothing to write down.

I looked over at Morris in his fishbowl. "You never get writer's bark. All you do all day is play in your fishbowl water."

I stood up and walked over to Morris's fishbowl. I picked up Morris's turtle food bottle next to his fishbowl. "Not only do you get to swim all day, but you also get to eat this yummy food. Let's see what you get to eat. It says here you get to eat fish mush, dried crickets, worms, and algae."

"How many times do I have to tell you to stop eating Morris's turtle food?" Mom laughed from my bedroom doorway.

"That's not even funny, Mom. That's so gross."

"What has you up so early?" Mom asked. "The school bus doesn't get here for another two hours."

"I wanted to write more about my pirates, but I have writer's bark."

"That's called writer's block, and I may be able to help."

I sat back down at my desk.

"What do you remember about the pirates from yesterday?" Mom asked.

"They lacked manners, they didn't go to bed on time, you didn't want to say the words 'sea hippopotamus' around them, and they didn't wash their socks often enough. Creepy crabs! I believe that did it!" Upside, downside, side to side, from the inside to the outside and all the way roundabout, the north wind blew strong. "Mom, the pirates are back!!!"

"Wonderful," Mom said. "I'll leave you alone with your pirate friends. I'm sure you have a lot to write about."

Mom left my room, closing the door behind her.

"Hello, Sparky," Gobble said. "Sorry, but all of us pirates are a little knackered."

"I'm sorry. I forgot pirates go to bed when the sun comes up. By the way, what does 'knackered' mean?"

"It means we put up a real hullabaloo all night long and now we're sleepy," Bobble said as he yawned.

"Hullabaloo sounds cool," I said. "Pirates sure know a lot about fun words."

"The sun is shining in our eyes, so it's time for us pirates to head to bed," Captain Wobble said.

"Wait, don't go to bed just yet. I need to write more about the pirate kind of stuff."

"We did give Sparky our word that we would teach her to be a pirate," Captain Wobble said.

"Pirates are known for not keeping their word," Gobble said.

"That's true," Bobble said.

"Hey, that's not nice," I said. "Being nice means you keep your word."

"We do want to be nice," Gobble said.

"That's true," Bobble said.

"Ok, we'll keep our word," Captain Wobble said. "We'll teach you to be a pirate."

"Great!" I said. "First, how do you know if you're a pirate or not?"

"You can smell a true pirate from a mile away," Bobble said.

"What do pirates smell like?" I asked.

"They smell like fish and chips," Bobble said.

"I bring Morris, my pet turtle, with me when I go to the pool," I said. "Will that help me smell like a pirate?"

"Whiff of a turtle is a lot like the smell of pirate's foot so that's close enough," Gobble said.

"But you can't just smell like a pirate to be a pirate," Captain Wobble said. "To be a pirate you must also look like a pirate. Do you want us to help you look like a pirate?"

"Yes, yes, and more yes! Please do make me look like a pirate!"

"100 days at sea and you'll be looking just like any sun-kissed merryman of a pirate," Gobble said.

"I don't have 100 days. I only have two hours before I leave for school."

"That could be a problem," Bobble said.

"I have a problem with a rock in my boot," Gobble said.

"I have a problem with a sea hippopotamus," Captain Wobble said.

"My problem is I don't look like a pirate," I said. "So what can I do about that?"

"Where do you keep your tusks from a sea hippopotamus?" Captain Wobble asked.

"I don't have any tusks from a sea hippopotamus," I said. "Why do I need them?"

"To cut your pants off at the knees," Captain Wobble said.

"Will a school scissors do?"

"It will have to do," Captain Wobble said.

I grabbed my favorite pair of pants out of my closet and pulled my scissors out of my backpack.

"Now cut your pants off at the knees," Captain Wobble said.

"Make sure to cut your pants off in wiggly lines," Gobble said. "Pirates are as crooked as a rusty hook."

I cut my pants off at the knees with a zig and a zag, then I held my pants in the air. "What do you think?"

"The tusks from a sea hippopotamus couldn't have done a better job," Captain Wobble said. "Now you need a shirt with holes in the sleeves."

"Why do I need holes in the sleeves of my shirt?" I asked.

"The claw snapping crabs are sure to make holes in the sleeves of any real pirate's shirt," Captain Wobble said.

I reached in my closet and pulled out my nicest silk shirt and cut holes in the sleeves.

"Now do I look like a pirate?"

"You're almost there, but something is missing," Gobble said. "I can't seem to put it into words."

"If I could spell better, I might be able to help," Bobble said.

"Sparky's shirt doesn't seem to say 'pirate,'" Captain Wobble said.

"I know just what to do." I pulled my black marker out of my backpack and wrote the word 'pirate' right across the front of my shirt in big letters.

"That's it!!" All three pirates cheered as they hooked arms and broke out in a dance.

"Wonderful! Now I'm going to look like a pirate," I said as I spun around like a top.

"Hold it right there," Captain Wobble said. "Sparky still needs pirate boots."

"Boots make the pirate," Gobble said.

I ran to my closet and pulled out my red rubber rain boots. "What do you think? Will these boots make the romping stomping sound of pirate boots?"

"What kind of boots are those?" Captain Wobble asked.

"They're my red rubber rain boots. They're called galoshes."

"I've never heard of a pirate wearing red rubber galoshes on their feet," Captain Wobble said.

"I'm afraid of getting my feet wet," I said.

"What!!! Pails of super silly sailing snails, I've never heard of such a thing," Captain Wobble said. "There has never been a pirate who doesn't dip her toes in the water every now and then."

"This is truly very odd," Bobble said. "Water on your toes as it goes is ever a pirate's lot."

"Don't tell me that," I said. "When water gets on my feet, it makes me think of wiggly slimy slugs slithering between my toes."

"Sparky, it's almost time for the school bus!" Mom hollered up to me from downstairs. "You need to eat your bagel."

"I'm still writing my pirate story!" I hollered back.

"Every good story has an ending!" Mom hollered back up to me. "I think the school bus just pulled up."

The north wind grew still, and I put my notebook, dictionary, and pencil into my backpack.

Chapter 5

Sparky Reads Her Story

I put on my pirate clothes, took off downstairs, grabbed grandma's cane that she forgot in the living room, and bolted into the kitchen.

"Why do you have grandma's cane, and what happened to your clothes?!!" Mom asked. "And why do you have 'pirate' written on your shirt?"

"Pirate ships are known for their rocky ride. Grandma's cane may come in handy." I grabbed the bagel out of the toaster and flew out the front door to the school bus.

"We're going to have a talk after school, young lady," Mom said from the front door. "Those were nice clothes."

"Mom, don't worry about me or my clothes," I yelled back as I jumped onto the school bus and stuck my head out the window. "Everything is going to be ok. I've become a pirate."

The school bus rumbled down the road, and the north wind blew as I pulled my pirate story out of my backpack. I started to write again.

Once I got to school, the fact that I might be a pirate jumped from kid to kid like fungus on a pirate's toe.

The north wind blew strong the whole school day. I wrote on my pirate story during recess. I wrote some more during lunch, and I wrote skipping down the hallway.

I made it to English class with my pirate story in hand.

"Who would like to read their story first?" Mrs. Chatafoola, my fourth-grade English teacher, asked.

"Let Sparky read her story first," Jill said as she raised her hand from the front of the class. "She's a pirate."

"I believe Sparky is the first pirate I've ever had in my English class," Mrs. Chatafoola said with a big smile.

"Sparky's not a pirate," Billy said without raising his hand.

"Sparky does have 'pirate' written on her shirt," Tony said.

"Anyone can have the word 'pirate' written on their shirt," Bucky said. "It doesn't mean they're a pirate."

"It doesn't mean they're not a pirate," Leo said.

"And why does Sparky have a cane in her hand?" Billy asked.

"Pirate ships make for a rocky ride," Jill said. "A cane could come in handy."

"Give me a break," Billy said.

"We want to hear Sparky's pirate story," the class chanted.

"Sparky, would you like to be the first student to read your story?" Mrs. Chatafoola asked.

"Sure," I said as I walked to the front of the class, twirling my cane with my red rubber galoshes squeaking all the way.

The north wind blew, and I opened my notebook. "The name of my somewhat true story is Captain Sparky and the Pool Pirates." I read how I met the pirates who came through the pool drain. I read how I was going to teach the pirates to be nice and how the pirates were going to teach me to be a pirate. I looked up at the class. "This is where my pirate adventure really begins."

From the back of the class, Bucky started waving his hand like a windmill.

"Sparky, hold your place," Mrs. Chatafoola said. "It looks like some of your classmates have questions."

The north wind grew still, and I shut my notebook.

"My dad's a plumber," Bucky said. "A water drain and pipe are too small for pirates to climb out of."

"Maybe the pirates do yoga," Jill said. "You can bend like a pretzel if you do yoga."

"An ant would have trouble climbing out of a pool drain!" Bucky said.

"There's no way Sparky's story can be somewhat true," Billy said. "And pirates aren't nice."

"Sparky's nice," Tony said.

"That's the whole point," Billy said. "Sparky isn't a pirate."

"We'll know if Sparky's a pirate before the ice cream melts," Leo said. "That's what my mom always says."

"Pirates, pirates, pirates," Sparky's English class chanted.

"Ok, class, please remain calm," Mrs. Chatafoola said. "Sparky, you can start reading your story again."

The north wind blew as I opened my notebook and began to read.

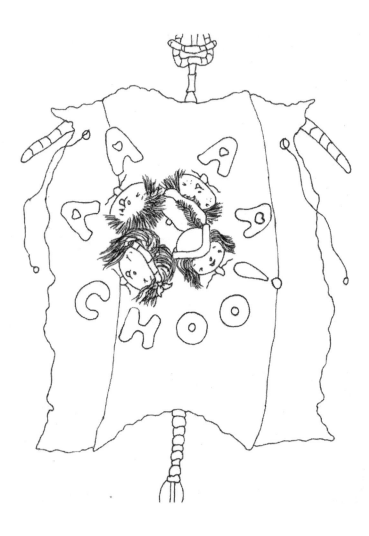

Chapter 6

Waiting for a Williwaw

So, there I was in the pool with three pirates who were eager to sail away.

"It's time to set sail," Captain Wobble said. "My pirate ship is anchored in the water pipes below."

"Hold on! I need my backpack," I said. "My notebook and pencil are in there."

"Be quick about it," Captain Wobble said. "The water won't stay wet forever."

I ran and grabbed my backpack from the pool locker room. With a double dip of my red rubber galoshes, I was back in the pool and ready for the adventures that lay head.

Down the drain Bobble, Gobble, Captain Wobble, and I all went. There it stood right before my eyes... a real honest to goodness pirate ship of a wreck.

"What do you think of my pirate ship?" Captain Wobble asked.

"This pirate ship looks like it's been chewed on by a dog. And it better float, because I don't."

"I think it floats, I hope it floats, it better float," Captain Wobble said. "I traded my whole seashell collection for this boat."

"So you're saying your pirate ship floats, right?" I asked.

"My pirate ship is made of wood and most wood floats," Captain Wobble said.

"Most wood floats or all wood floats?" I asked. "Because floating and not floating aren't the same thing."

"All aboard," Captain Wobble said. "Everybody watch your heads. The water pipes make for a tight fit."

"You didn't actually answer my question about the floating part," I said loudly.

"There's no time to waste," Captain Wobble said as all the pirates started climbing the ropes to board the pirate ship.

"Oh brother, help me," I said. I was the last one to climb the ropes and board the pirate ship.

"Here, wear this," Captain Wobble said, handing me a lifejacket. "This will help you to float."

"Thanks," I said as I put the lifejacket on.

All three pirates grew very still on the pirate ship deck.

"What's going on?" I asked Captain Wobble.

"We're waiting," Captain Wobble said.

"Waiting for what?" I asked.

"We're waiting for a williwaw to catch our sails," Captain Wobble said.

"Do you get many williwaws down here in the water pipes?" I asked.

"Almost never," Captain Wobble said.

"Are you kidding me?" I said. "We could be down here waiting forever for a williwaw that never comes."

"Well, do you have any better of an idea?" Captain Wobble asked.

"As a matter of fact, I think I do. What if we fill our cheeks with air and blow into the sails? It may not be a williwaw, but it might be just what we need to get this pirate ship moving."

"That does sound like a good idea," Captain Wobble said. "Let's give it a try."

"Ok, everybody, on the count of three we fill our cheeks with air and blow at the sails," I said.

"One… two…. three!" The pirates and I all blew into the sails, but the ship didn't move an inch.

"Nice try, Sparky," Captain Wobble said. "But it looks like we're going to have to wait for a williwaw."

"If only we had a pepper shaker," I said.

"I have a pepper shaker," Gobble said as he pulled a pepper shaker from his pocket and handed it to me.

"Why, may I ask, do you keep a pepper shaker in your pocket?"

"You never know when a plumb bug will come crawling by," Gobble said. "Black pepper makes anything tasty."

"Whoever said you can't ask too many questions was wrong, but the good news is now we may be able to make our own williwaw."

"How so?" Captain Wobble asked.

"Just follow my lead. Now on the count of three, I'm going to toss all the pepper in the air, we'll all take a good whiff, then everybody sneeze at the sails."

I took the lid off the pepper shaker and tossed the pepper into the air. Then it happened. One sneeze.

Two sneezes. Three sneezes. And then many more sneezes.

"SNEEZE AT THE SAILS!!!" I yelled out.

The pirate ship rocked back and forth as our sneezes caught the sails. With a rush of sneezing, the pirate ship took off down the water pipes and into the open sea.

"We're off," Captain Wobble said.

"I have a problem!" Billy shouted from his classroom seat.

The north wind grew still, and I stopped reading.

"Billy, if you have a question for Sparky, ask nicely," Mrs. Chatafoola said.

"This can't be a somewhat true story," Billy said. "It's simply not possible to sneeze hard enough into a pirate ship's sail to move a pirate ship."

"Have you ever tried to sneeze into a pirate ship's sail?" Jill asked. "I didn't think so."

"You must remember the pirate ship is in the water pipes," Tony said. "The wind is stronger in the water pipes because it has only one place to go—out the other end."

"Tony may have a point," Leo said.

"Tony doesn't have a point," Billy said.

"None of this makes a lick of sense," Bucky said.

"Ok, class, let Sparky get back to reading her story," Mrs. Chatafoola said.

The north wind blew, and I began to read.

Chapter 7

Sailing to Wherever

"Where are we sailing to?" I asked Captain Wobble as the pirate ship roared through the open sea.

"We're sailing to nowhere," Captain Wobble said.

"If you're sailing to nowhere, you'll never get anywhere," I said.

"Not true," Captain Wobble said. "I find if you sail to nowhere, you always end up somewhere."

"Somewhere is everywhere," I said. "But most likely not where you want to be."

"Also not true," Captain Wobble said. "Some places you end up at makes sailing there all the more worth it."

"I see. Sailing to nowhere is like sailing a little to the left, a little to the right, and somewhere down the middle. In the end, you may end up right where you want to be."

"You're exactly right," Captain Wobble said.

"I just wish I knew what exactly I was right about."

"Keep the sails steady," Captain Wobble said. "The last place we want to end up at is elsewhere."

As we sailed along, the pirates taught me about the surf, swell, foam, suds, rollers, breakers, and white caps. I began to fall in love with the sea just like the pirates.

The wind slowed down and the pirate ship came to a gentle roll.

"Time for a swim!" shouted Captain Wobble as he jumped overboard.

"Cannonball!" Bobble yelled as he jumped overboard.

"Look at me!" Gobble yelled as he did three flips off the deck and dove into the water.

With my lifejacket on, I stayed safely aboard the pirate ship and watched the pirates swimming about.

Five minutes later, things changed fast. Gobble, Bobble, and Captain Wobble climbed back onto the ship crying with crabs hanging all over them.

"Sparky! Get the crabs off us!!! Get them off!!!" Bobble and Gobble cried.

"It hurts!" Captain Wobble cried.

"Hold your seahorses. I'll pull the crabs off each one of you, but there's only one of me."

After an hour of pulling crabs off the pirates, I finally pulled the last crab off Bobble's nose.

"Those crabs are nasty," Captain Wobble said as he wiped away a tear.

"Those pinching crabs are mean," Gobble said with a scrunched-up nose and a frowny face.

"It's true, crabs are crabby through and through," I said. "But pinching is just what crabs most like to do and since your pirates, you should know that."

"I have the right mind to bite the next crab that ever pinches me again," Bobble said.

"You do that and you'll end up with a crab hanging on the end of your nose again." Before I could say another word, a huge williwaw hit the ship's sails.

"Man the sails!" Captain Wobble shouted. "We're off again."

"Which direction should we point the sails?" Bobble and Gobble asked.

"Let me guess," I said. "We're sailing to wherever."

"Point the sails to wherever," Captain Wobble bellowed. "It's as good a place as any other."

We sailed, sailed, and sailed some more, but it didn't look like we were going to reach wherever anytime soon.

As the pirate ship sailed along, the moon snuck a piggyback ride on the incoming waves and now it was my bedtime.

"Look at me!" Bobble shouted. "I can stand on my tippy toes and slap both knees at the same time."

"Check this out!" Gobble yelled as he leaped in the air and landed in the splits.

"Isn't this fun?" Captain Wobble yelled out as he did a cartwheel and landed on his bottom.

Bobble, Gobble, and Captain Wobble were acting crazier than a pack of penguins at a fish market. I was never going to get any sleep.

"Aren't you sleepy?" I asked the pirates.

"No, not even a little," Captain Wobble said. "Pirates do their best pirating at night."

"I forgot pirates like to stay up all night long, but I like to sleep all night long. Why don't you pirates all go to bed? You might stub a toe in the dark."

"It's ok if we hurt one toe. We still have nine other toes that will do the job just fine," Gobble said.

It was hopeless, but then an idea came to me. When my mom wants me to fall asleep, she tells me a story, and then sure enough I'm out like a light in no time at all.

"Look at us!" the pirates shouted as they leapfrogged over each other and landed in one big heap.

"Sleepy squid squeezes! I have just the bedtime story for you," I hollered loud enough to be heard above all the pirates' knee-slapping and boot-stomping monkey-romping.

"I like stories," Bobble said.

"Me, too," Gobble said.

"Everybody, take a seat," Captain Wobble said. "Let's hear Sparky's story."

Chapter 8

The Squirrel, Dog, and Bird

"I'm going to tell you a story just like my mom tells me before bed," I said.

"Is it a scary story?" Bobble asked. "Because scary stories keep me up."

"No, it's not a scary story," I said.

"Is it a story about a shark?" Gobble asked. "Sharks aren't nice."

"No, it's not a story about a shark," I said.

"I don't think I like your story," Captain Wobble said.

"I haven't even started telling you my story yet!!!" I said.

"You shouldn't talk so loud," Bobble said. "It's hard to sleep when people talk loud."

"That's very true," Gobble said.

"I'm hungry," Captain Wobble said.

I gritted my teeth and spoke in a low voice. "Everybody chill out and let me tell my story."

"Hip hip hooray! We get to hear a story!" the pirates cheered.

I shook my head, blew out a hot puff of air, and started to tell my story. "There once was a squirrel who wanted to be a pirate. She spent all day climbing trees. There was a dog who wanted to be a pirate. He spent all day digging up bones. There was a bird who wanted to be a pirate. He spent all day with his head buried in the sand."

"I like to dig up dinosaur bones," Gobble said as he leaned his head on a barrel.

"Gobble, that's a little creepy, but thank you for sharing," I said.

"Does the bird chirp?" Bobble asked as he rested his head in his hands.

"Most birds do chirp," I said. "So the bird in my story chirps."

"I wish I were a squirrel," Captain Wobble said as he leaned back onto the wooden beam.

"That's something to wish for, I guess. Now the bird, dog, and squirrel didn't get along and were never nice to each other."

"That's too bad," Captain Wobble said.

"That makes me sad," Gobble said.

"Were the bird, dog, and squirrel mad at each other?" Bobble asked.

"If you let me finish my story, you might find out," I said.

"Sorry," Captain Wobble said. "Please carry on."

"Please do," Gobble said.

"Yes, please do," Bobble said.

"Ok, now the squirrel would climb to the top of a walnut tree. When the dog or bird walked under the walnut tree, the squirrel would drop walnuts on their heads."

"That sounds like it would hurt," Captain Wobble said.

"My head hurts already," Bobble said.

"I like walnuts," Gobble said. "Does anyone else like walnuts?"

I put both hands on my head. "Most people like walnuts!"

"I don't like walnuts," Bobble said.

"Can we PLEASE stop talking about walnuts and could you let me finish my story!!!"

"What was the story about again?" Bobble asked. "I forgot."

"I think Sparky's story was about ducks," Gobble said.

"That's right, Sparky's story is about ducks," Captain Wobble said.

"My story is not about ducks!"

"I don't think you're telling your story right because ducks go 'quack' not 'chirp,'" Bobble said.

"Quack, quack, quack," went all three pirates.

My fingers flared out like claws. My lips peeled back and you could see all my teeth. A lion growl came from down under.

"We've never had someone nice enough to tell us a story," Gobble said with a yawn.

"That's why we like you so much, Sparky, because you're nice," Bobble said with a yawn all of his own.

I was about to scream, but I put my hand over my mouth. I was supposed to be teaching the pirates to be nice. I had to let it go. I must remain clam. My lips came down and hid my teeth again. I shook my hands and let them hang loose. With much work, my lion growl turned into a whisper.

"Are you finished with your story?" Captain Wobble asked with a stretch from head to toe.

"I think Sparky is finished with her story," Gobble said.

"Sparky's story was the best story I've ever heard," Bobble said.

"I just want you to know that I'm trying very hard to hold it together, and no, I'm not finished with my story."

"Ok, we want to hear the rest of your story," all the pirates said as their eyelids fluttered about like a duck feather caught in a williwaw.

I cracked my knuckles and picked up my story where I left off. "The bird would never say a word to the squirrel or the dog. He would just bury his head in the sand."

"You shouldn't bury your head in the sand. I tried it once and got sand in my ears," Gobble said.

"Gobble, burying your head in the sand doesn't make any sense," I said.

"Not even if you're a pirate?" Gobble asked.

"NO!!! Not even if you're a pirate," I said.

"Can I say one last thing about the bird?" Bobble asked.

"One last thing," I said. "And that's it."

"That bird is rude," Bobble said. "You shouldn't bury your head in the sand when people are around."

"That's very true," Captain Wobble said.

"NO ONE FOR ANY REASON SHOULD EVER BURY THEIR HEAD IN THE SAND!!! Now I'm going to finish my story, and I don't care how long it takes. One day the dog was walking by the walnut tree when a mighty wind blew the squirrel out of the tree."

"Did the dog bite the squirrel's tail?" Bobble asked.

"No, the dog didn't bite the squirrel's tail!" I said. "What kind of story do you think this is?"

"I thought this wasn't a scary story," Captain Wobble said.

"Scary stories keep me awake," Bobble said.

"Me, too," Gobble said.

"LIKE I SAID OVER AND OVER AGAIN!!! This isn't a scary story." I felt myself unrolling like a ball of yarn in a kitten's mouth.

"Could you whisper? I'm sleepy," Bobble said as he closed his eyes.

"I'm sleepy, too," Gobble said as he closed his eyes.

"I'm happy and sleepy," Captain Wobble said as he closed his eyes.

"WHAT'S THE MATTER WITH YOU PIRATES?" I asked. "Telling a story to pirates is like telling a story to a kindergartener who ate marshmallows for dinner then stuffed cupcakes up his nose."

That's when I heard a snore, then another snore, and then one more snore. That's three snores for three pirates if my fourth-grade math is correct.

The pirates were all asleep, but I was so worked up I felt like I needed to run on a hamster wheel. That's when I heard a GRUNT, GRUNT, GRUNT sailing by with the sea breeze.

I took tiny steps all the way to the side of the pirate ship, then took a quick peek overboard. For one click of the clock, I swore I saw two twitching ears and two big and round baby soft eyes looking back at me.

I rubbed my eyes and then all I saw was sea water. Could that have been the sea hippopotamus that the pirates were telling me about? I must be seeing things. It was time for bed for sure.

The night time sea breeze was chilly, and I had a plan for that pirate flag flapping above my head. I lowered the pirate flag with the ropes. Lying down, I wrapped myself up in the flag to keep warm. Now you can make that four snores for four pirates.

"I have a question!" Billy shouted from his classroom seat.

The north wind grew still, and I stopped reading.

Chapter 9

The Stolen Pirate Flag

"Billy, you can ask Sparky a question, but please, use your soft voice," Mrs. Chatafoola said.

"Hippos only live in rivers, lakes, or swamps, not seas," Billy said.

"If you're a sea hippopotamus, you can live in a sea," Jill said.

"I'll say it again," Billy said. "There simply are no sea hippos."

"Pirates would know if there's a sea hippopotamus or not," Tony said.

"Sparky's not a pirate!" Bucky said.

"At this point, we can't be sure if Sparky is or isn't a pirate," Leo said.

"Yes, we do know for sure!" Bucky said. "Sparky is a fourth grader like the rest of us. Fourth graders can't be pirates."

"My mom called my three-year-old sister a little pirate just the other day," Jill said.

"That doesn't make your little sister or Sparky a real pirate!" Billy said.

"Sparky, you can start reading your story again," Mrs. Chatafoola said.

The north wind blew, and I began to read.

The next day I woke up with a jump as panicky pirates were running to and fro all across the ship deck. "What's going on?"

"The pirate flag is missing off the jackstaff," Captain Wobble shouted.

"What in the world is a jackstaff?" I asked.

"It's the flagpole on a ship," Captain Wobble said as he looked to be falling apart faster than a pirate ship with dry rot caught in a williwaw.

I looked over to where I was sleeping. I could see the pirate flag all wrapped up in a ball in the corner of the deck. "Captain Wobble, there's something I must tell you. I used the..."

"No time to talk," Captain Wobble said, cutting in. "Pirates must have come aboard our ship in the middle of the night and swiped my pirate flag right from under our noses."

"What's the big deal about a pirate flag?" I asked, thinking I might have done something really bad.

"What's the big deal about a pirate flag?!" Captain Wobble said. "Without a pirate flag, a pirate ship is just a ship, and a pirate is just a sailor. When we find out who took my pirate flag, a sea hippopotamus is going to have a full belly, let me tell you."

This may not be the time to tell the pirates I took the pirate flag to keep warm last night. I very carefully walked over to the corner of the ship deck where I slept. I took a look around to make sure none of the pirates were looking my way. I picked up the pirate flag and stuffed it into my backpack.

"We're all doomed to be just sailors, yes, just sailors," the pirates cried out.

Things didn't look good. Bobble, Gobble, and Captain Wobble were cracking faster than crab legs on a pirate's dinner plate.

"Slurping fish noodles!" I said. "I can fix your pirate flag problem!"

The pirates came to a stop right on the spot and yelled out, "Hark, hark, hark!"

"What does 'hark' mean?" I asked.

"It means to listen," Captain Wobble said.

"Great, because I want you to listen," I said. "I have a good idea."

I carefully reached into the bottom of my backpack and pulled out my white gym shirt. "How about we make this t-shirt into a pirate flag?"

"A pirate flag is very special," Captain Wobble said. "It won't be easy to make one."

"Let me give it a good twirly whirly," I said. "What do you say?"

Captain Wobble wiggled his nose from right to left, then stopped it in the middle. "I say we give it a twirly whirly."

I pulled out a black marker from my backpack. "Let's get started."

"You'll need to draw something on that t-shirt with the winking eyes of a pirate," Captain Wobble said. "Nothing else will do."

"I like bones," Gobble said.

"How about we draw something with fangs," Bobble said.

"How about I draw a kitty cat," I said.

"Aren't kitties fluffy and cute?" Bobble asked.

"I've never met a fluffy and cute pirate," Captain Wobble said.

"You want people to think you are nice pirates, right?" I asked.

"We do want people to think we're nice," Gobble said.

"That is true," Bobble said.

"I've made up my mind," Captain Wobble said. "We go with a kitty cat on the new pirate flag."

With my black marker I drew a kitty cat on my t-shirt and lifted it into the air. "What do you think?"

"I've never seen a pirate flag like it," Gobble said.

"I think being nice takes a little getting used to," Bobble said.

"Don't you like the flag?" I asked.

Captain Wobble rubbed his chin. "I like it. Gobble and Bobble, waste no time, up to the top of the jackstaff with the new pirate flag."

Gobble and Bobble tied my kitty cat pirate flag to the jackstaff ropes and raised it to the top.

I looked up proudly at the pirate flag I had made as it flapped in the wind.

"We're no longer sailors but pirates once again, and our ship is now a pirate ship once more," Captain Wobble said. "We owe it all to you, Sparky."

"You're welcome," I said, feeling rather sneaky about the whole thing. As soon as I got the chance, I'd put the real pirate flag back up the jackstaff and nobody would be the wiser.

For the rest of the day, we played pirate games like who could make the best crab face, who could puff up their cheeks bigger than a blowfish, who could juggle the most coconuts, and we ran around the ship deck chasing the sea waves. We kept up all the fun until the giant clam in the sky swallowed the sun.

"I'm tired," Gobble said.

"Me, too," Bobble said.

"I don't think us pirates have ever been this tired at night," Captain Wobble said.

"I know pirates like to sleep during the day and romp about at night, but doesn't it seem more fun to do the pirate kind of stuff in the sunshine instead of in the darkness?"

"You can see plumb bugs better during the day," Gobble said.

"It's easier to find things like gold and silver in the daylight," Bobble said.

"The sun is shiny," Captain Wobble said with a yawn. "I like shiny things."

All three pirates and I found our spots on the ship deck and fell asleep.

Chapter 10
Jerky Turkey Island

Morning came with a jolt. I grabbed my cane and steadied myself as I watched the pirates tumble about the ship deck. "Golly poppers! What's wrong with the ship?"

"We hit something big," Captain Wobble said as he got to his feet.

"We've hit something that's not water," Bobble said.

"Did we reach nowhere or somewhere or over there or over here?" I asked. "I think only pirates can find these places on a map."

"We made it to elsewhere," Captain Wobble said.

"And that's not good, right?" I asked.

"Not good at all," Captain Wobble said. "We've run aground."

"What does 'run aground' mean?" I asked.

"It means that half the pirate ship is floating in the water and the other half is on the beach," Gobble said.

We all climbed off the ship and stood on the beach.

"Something doesn't seem right," Bobble said.

"Something doesn't seem right at all," Gobble said.

"Now what's wrong?" I asked.

"Take a look at the finger paintings on those trees up ahead," Captain Wobble said.

"They look like pictures of turkeys," I said.

"That's because they are pictures of turkeys," Captain Wobble said. "We've run aground on Jerky Turkey Island."

The pirates all shivered, but I laughed. "Jerky Turkey sounds silly."

"I'll show you silly," a voice boomed out from the jungle in front of us.

We all looked up to see flocks and lots of turkeys coming out of the jungle onto the beach.

"It's the Jerky Turkeys," Captain Wobble said as the pirates fell to their knees in fear.

"You better shake," a turkey said, stepping forward. This turkey wore a gold nugget necklace and a crown with a single pearl.

"Please spare us, turkey!" Captain Wobble cried out.

"That's King Fry to you," the turkey with the crown said.

"All hail King Fry," the rest of the turkeys chanted.

I chuckled.

"You think something's funny?" King Fry asked.

"It's nothing," I said.

"No, please do tell me what's so funny," King Fry said.

"All hail King Fry," the turkeys chanted again.

I started giggling. "It's just that your name is King Fry."

The turkeys all looked at each other.

"Get it? Fry, like as in deep fry," I said.

"So, you're a funny girl," King Fry snarled. "You want to see funny? I'll show you funny."

"Big whippy do to you," I said as I pushed out my bottom lip. "You don't scare me."

King Fry puffed up his chest feathers. "We'll see about that."

Captain Wobble jumped to his feet. "She didn't mean anything by it. Forgive her. She's just a wee little one."

"Did I ask you to speak?" King Fry asked.

"I'm so sorry, so very sorry," Captain Wobble said. "She didn't mean anything by it, honest."

"You turkeys need to watch your manners," I said.

King Fry came over to me.

"What's your problem?" I asked. "How about you just chill—OOOUCH!!!" I said as King Fry pecked me on the top of the head. "That wasn't very nice!"

"That's good, because we're not very nice turkeys," King Fry sneered.

"You could learn a lot about being nice from my pirate friends," I said.

"Pirates aren't nice," King Fry said. "Pirates are almost as nasty as us turkeys."

"Not these pirates," I said, pointing at Bobble, Gobble, and Captain Wobble. "They're the first nice pirates that have ever lived."

"Look at our pirate flag. It has a kitten on it," Bobble said. "We're as nice as kitty cats."

"Really, so you're nice pirates?" King Fry sneered along with the rest of his pack of birdies.

"That's right," I said. "These pirates are nice pirates."

"I can see you've run your pirate ship aground on my beach," King Fry said. "Pirates catch landlubber fever and go bonkers the longer they're away from the sea. You pirates will turn on each other for sure."

"Not these pirates," I said. "They're full of kitty cat snuggles and cuddles."

King Fry and all his birdies broke out into mad laughter.

"There's not a pirate here who won't have a full-blown case of landlubber fever by morning," King Fry said. "All pirates turn nasty the longer they're away from the rolling of the sea waves."

"We'll see about that," I said. "These pirates are more nice than nasty for sure."

King Fry shook his feathers. "I'll tell you what. We'll come back tomorrow morning, and if you pirates are more nice than nasty, we'll let you go. But if you're more nasty than nice, we'll peck holes in your ship and you'll be stuck here forever."

"Fine," I said. "We'll take your more nasty than nice test."

King Fry and his birdies laughed and chuckled as they walked back into the jungle of palm trees.

"Too bad you turkeys just picked the losing ticket!" I yelled after King Fry. "We'll be out of this place first thing in the morning for sure."

Chapter 11

Landlubber Fever

"Sparky, there's something we need to tell you," Captain Wobble said.

"Tell me what?" I asked.

"You see, pirates are made for the sea and the sea is for pirates. A pirate that is stuck on land will get landlubber fever in short order."

"Surly you can all last one night on land?" I asked.

"I miss the sea already," Bobble said as he flashed his teeth. "I think I want to bite someone."

"Captain Wobble, do you mind if I take a look at your gold fillings?" Gobble asked. "You can never have enough gold."

"Nice try, but my gold fillings are staying where they belong... in my mouth," Captain Wobble said as he closed his mouth and talked through his teeth. "I think I'm looking at a bunch of plank walkers."

"Stop," I said. "Landlubber fever is starting already. You only have till tomorrow morning, and we will all be sailing again."

"Morning seems like such a long time away," Gobble said. "Did I just hear the jingle of silver coins in someone's pocket?"

Crumbling crab cakes! Landlubber fever was in full moon bloom. "Wait! The sea is right in front of us. What if we play in the water and build sandcastles? It might help us get over landlubber fever."

"I can hear the waves calling my name," Captain Wobble said.

"Last one in the water is a rotten egg!" Bobble yelled out.

All the pirates and I took off our boots and tossed them in the air. The pirates ran into the water, but I came to a stop right at the water's edge.

"Come on in," Gobble said as he splashed around.

"It's loads of fun," Bobble said as he skipped through the waves. "I feel the landlubber fever leaving me already."

"Look at me! I can wiggle my lips like a fish tail," Captain Wobble said. "What are you waiting for, Sparky? You're missing all the monkeyshines."

"I can't get my feet wet. I just can't."

"Why?" Captain Wobble asked. "You were right. Playing in the waves is a cure for landlubber fever."

"I'm just too afraid of getting my feet wet," I said, looking down at the sand. "I guess I'll never truly be a pirate."

"You're about as much a pirate as anyone could be," Captain Wobble said. "All you have to do is wet your toes and a pirate you'll be forevermore."

Billy popped out of his classroom seat and pointed his finger at me.

The north wind grew still, and I stopped reading my story.

"Billy, do you have a question for Sparky?" Mrs. Chatafoola asked.

"Sparky's not a pirate, and her story can't be somewhat true," Billy said with his finger still pointing at me. "There has never been a pirate that has ever lived that didn't get his or her feet wet."

"Billy, I thought you didn't believe in pirates," Jill said.

"I don't," Billy said.

"I don't believe in pirates either," Bucky said.

"I believe in pirates," Tony said.

"You probably believe in unicorns, too," Billy said.

"How did you know I believe unicorns?" Tony asked.

"I need to find a new school," Billy said as he threw his hands in the air.

"Maybe Sparky gets her feet wet, maybe she doesn't," Leo said. "But I would like to find out."

"That's a good point," Mrs. Chatafoola said. "Sparky, you can start reading your story again."

The north wind blew, and I started reading my story.

There I was at the edge of the water, looking at the rolling of the waves. I watched Bobble, Gobble, and Captain Wobble having as much fun as three otters in a goldfish bowl.

"I'm brave." I took a step. "I'm fearless." I took another step. "I'm plucky by golly!" I yelled out as I jumped into the deep blue sea. With my lifejacket still on and the water almost up to my ankles, I knew now that I was meant to be a pirate.

"Look!!" Gobble said. "Sparky got her feet wet. She's a pirate like us now."

"It's true," Bobble said. "Sparky is a pirate and a nice one, too."

"Sparky, it's your pirate flag that's blowing in the wind atop my pirate ship so that makes you as much a pirate captain as me," Captain Wobble said.

"You mean I'm not just a pirate, I'm a pirate captain?"

"Yes," Captain Wobble said, smiling from cheek to cheek. "It looks like there are two pirate captains on my ship now."

"Captain Sparky, we're at your service," Bobble and Gobble said with a bow.

"My first order I'm going to give as a pirate captain is that we keep having loads of fun!!!"

"Hip hip hooray!!! Hip hip hooray!!!" all the pirates and I cheered as we danced on the beach.

This was by far the best day of my life.

The fun went on all day as we jumped over sea waves, collected seashells, built sandcastles, and chased crabs up and down the beach. The sun's gold shine now gave way to the moon's silver glow.

We all left the water and climbed onto the beach.

"I feel great," Gobble said.

"Me, too," Bobble said.

"Captain Sparky's idea of playing in the water did the trick," Captain Wobble said. "There's no sign of landlubber fever in any one of us."

"And you pirates are by far more nice than nasty," I said. "King Fry will have to let us go."

"We'll be back to sailing the sea by morning for sure," all three pirates cheered.

"Bobble, could you toss me my backpack? It's right beside you. I need to get out a pair of dry gym socks."

Bobble tossed my backpack to me. When the backpack hit my hands, the pirate flag that I had taken rolled out onto the beach. If ever anyone was caught in a crab's claw, it was me. My sneaky deed was now in the open.

"What's this?" Captain Wobble asked as he snatched up the pirate flag before I could.

"I think I've seen that pirate flag before," Gobble said.

"It looks a lot like Captain Wobble's pirate flag," Bobble said.

"That's because it is my pirate flag," Captain Wobble said. "Captain Sparky, it was you who took my pirate flag all along."

"I was cold last night, and I used it to keep warm, honest. I just didn't know how to tell you. I was going to put it back."

"I smell a pirate's foot," Gobble said.

"Sparky's one sneaky trickster for sure," Bobble said.

"All this time you were supposed to be teaching us to be nice," Captain Wobble said. "Instead, you were planning to overthrow my pirate ship and steal my crew."

"What are you talking about? Why would I want to do that? I just used your pirate flag to keep warm."

"It sounds to me like you were a pirate all along, just not a nice one," Captain Wobble said.

"You were playing us for fools," Gobble said.

"And we trusted you," Bobble said. "We should have known to never trust another pirate."

"FINE, ALL PIRATES ARE JUST SILLY AND FOOLISH!!! I don't know why I wanted to be a pirate in the first place." I marched down the beach far away from the pirates.

I laid down for the night sniffling and sad. It got colder as the night went on and the sea breeze made me shake and shiver. I just wanted to sail all the way home and forget about the pirates for good.

Chapter 12

The Sea Hippopotamus

Morning came and I awoke to a kind-sounding voice.

"Did you stay warm last night?" Captain Wobble asked.

I looked up at Bobble, Gobble, and Captain Wobble. They were all smiling at me...well at least as best as pirates could smile.

"Did my pirate flag keep you warm last night?" Captain Wobble asked.

"Yikes!!!" I yelled as I threw off the pirate flag that somehow got wrapped around me. "I swear I don't know how your pirate flag got wrapped around me. You've got to believe me."

"Don't worry," Captain Wobble said. "The sea breeze was chilly last night and Bobble, Gobble, and I put my pirate flag around you to keep you warm."

"But I thought you were mad at me for taking the pirate flag?" I asked.

"You have been nothing but nice to us, and no one has ever been nice to us before," Bobble said.

"You believe me about using the pirate flag to stay warm?" I asked.

"Yes, we believe you," Bobble and Gobble said.

"We trust you," Captain Wobble said. "Well as much as a pirate can be trusted."

"You guys are the best," I said.

"If you ever get cold again, you can use my pirate flag to keep warm anytime you want," Captain Wobble said.

"Wrapping me up in your pirate flag to keep me warm is the nicest thing anyone has ever done for me," I said.

"Who's nice?" I heard King Fry say with a rough voice as all the Jerky Turkeys came out of the jungle and onto the beach.

"Well, if it isn't King Fry and his pack of birdies," I said. "Sorry to upset you, but not only did these pirates overcome landlubber fever, but they were also nice to me."

"I don't believe it," King Fry said. "There's no such thing as a nice pirate."

"Then you're looking at the world's first nice pirates," I said. "Bobble, Gobble, and Captain

Wobble wrapped me in a pirate flag last night to keep me warm."

"Ooooooooooh, these pirates are nice pirates," all of King Fry's pack of birdies said. "We must keep our word and not peck holes in their pirate ship."

"Fine, I'll keep my word," King Fry said. "But by the looks of your pirate ship, you're not going anywhere any time soon. Good luck sailing on land."

"King Fry, you stop right there," I said. "These pirates were more nice than nasty. You have to keep your word like your pack of birdies said and let us go."

King Fry stuck his tongue out and wiggled it at me. "I said we wouldn't peck holes in your ship if you were more nice than nasty. Sorry to tell you, but getting your ship back into the water is your problem."

"Let me at him!!!" I shouted as my fellow pirates held me back. "I'll snap him like a wishbone."

"I'm so scared," King Fry sneered. "How about I peck you on the nose?"

"How about I pluck all your feathers out one by one?" I growled.

"Come and get it," King Fry said.

"I think I'm going to cook me up some roasted turkey!" I snarled.

"Just leave her alone," Captain Wobble said as he stepped in front of me, trying to give me a chance to cool down.

"Enjoy your stay on Jerky Turkey Island," King Fry said as he and his pack of birdies walked back into the jungle, laughing all the way.

"The curse of an octopus hug has fallen on us," Captain Wobble said. "King Fry's right. We'll never get off this island with half the pirate ship stuck on the beach."

"There's no way we're going to be able to push the pirate ship back into the sea," Gobble said.

"It looks like landlubber fever is going to get us one way or another," Bobble said.

"Maybe not," I said as I pulled out from my pocket a soggy, two-week-old, half of a chocolate chip cookie that I had been saving. "We have this."

"That looks like a waterlogged half of a chocolate chip cookie." Captain Wobble said. "I hope you have something else in your pocket. Like a tugboat."

"I'll show you the power of the cookie," I said. "Just give me a chance and you'll see."

"I think the sun might be getting to you," Captain Wobble said. "Let's get you into the shade."

"It's just horrible, I tell you, just horrible," Bobble sniffled. "We'll never get off Jerky Turkey Island, I tell you, never."

"We'll see about that," I said as I put my lifejacket back on and walked up to where the beach met the sea. I began waving the cookie in the air. "Come and get it, come and get it."

"If only things could stop getting any worse," Gobble cried out. "Sparky has a full-blown case of landlubber fever."

"Come and get it, come and get it," I yelled again. Then two soft round eyes and two twitching ears appeared in the water just ten feet out and began moving towards me.

"It's a sea hippopotamus!" screamed Gobble.

"We're all doomed!" Bobble cried out in tears.

"Run to the jungle!" Captain Wobble shouted.

"Hold your ground," I yelled out. "I know what I'm doing."

I waved the chocolate chip cookie in the air as the two soft round eyes and the two twitching ears stopped only five feet from the beach. Step by step, I walked into the water closer and closer to the sea hippopotamus.

"No," Bobble cried from behind me. "I can't watch."

"Sparky was the best pirate to have ever lived," Gobble said. "And now it's over."

"Come back to us before it's too late!" Captain Wobble shouted out.

"Just trust me!" I yelled back as I stopped knee-deep in the water and reached out my hand with the cookie. "Come on, take the cookie." The sea hippopotamus came all the way up to me and nibbled on the cookie while it was still in my hand.

"It's only a baby sea hippopotamus," Gobble laughed.

"The scary sea hippopotamus is cute and cuddly," Bobble said.

"Are you all thinking what I'm thinking?" Captain Wobble asked with a smile.

"That it would be nice to have cookies and milk right now?" Gobble said.

"Cookies and milk would be nice, but no," Captain Wobble said. "I'm thinking Sparky may have found us the help we need to get off this nasty island."

"Get ready to set sail," I said. "Everyone to the front of the pirate ship and push."

All of the pirates and I ran to the front of the pirate ship that was still stuck on the beach and pushed.

"Come on, little cutie," I said to the baby sea hippopotamus who had made his way onto the beach. "Don't go back into the sea just yet. We need your help."

All the pirates and I kept pushing the pirate ship with all our might.

"It isn't budging an inch," Captain Wobble said. "We need that baby hippopotamus's help."

"Just keep pushing," I said. "Come on, little hippopotamus. We need your help."

The sea hippopotamus tilted his head, then walked up to the front of the pirate ship right next to us.

"I think the baby hippopotamus is getting the idea," Captain Wobble said.

The baby sea hippopotamus laid his strong forehead onto the pirate ship's front beam and started pushing with the rest of us.

"Come on, baby hippopotamus," Gobble said.

"You can do it, little hippopotamus," Bobble said.

"Everybody give it one big push," I said.

With the help of the baby hippopotamus, the pirate ship began to creak and rock as it slid back into the sea.

"The pirate ship is free!!" Captain Wobble yelled out. "Everyone on board before it floats away."

We all climbed the ropes and boarded the pirate ship. We were at sea once again.

The baby sea hippopotamus followed the ship from behind as we sailed far away from Jerky Turkey Island.

Chapter 13

Is the Story True?

With the homeward bound williwaw blowing in our favor, we reached the pool pipes in no time at all.

"This is your stop," Captain Wobble said.

"Aren't you all coming with me?" I asked.

"We need to go back to the sea," Captain Wobble said. "I think there's a baby sea hippopotamus that needs help finding it's mommy and daddy."

"That's so nice," I said with a tear running down my cheek. "I'm sorry for crying."

"Don't be sorry for crying," Captain Wobble said. "If you didn't cry every now and then, you would fill up with water and float away."

"I love you guys," I said sniffling up tears. "Don't stay away for long."

"We won't. Now off you go," Captain Wobble said.

I hugged each pirate, then climbed down the pirate ship rope. "Hey, there are two water pipes. Which one should I take?"

"Don't take the pipe on the right," Gobble said. "It leads to the toilet."

"Trust me," Bobble said. "You don't want to take that one."

"I'll remember that," I said. "Should I take the pipe on the left?"

"That's the one I would take!" Captain Wobble said as the pirate ship caught a williwaw and zoomed away.

Up the left pipe I went, and with one big push I popped out of the pool drain. Now I have two homes and two loves. One on land and one that floats in the open sea.

The north wind twirled all around me, then sailed away. I closed my notebook.

"Wow, Sparky, that was one wonderful story," Mrs. Chatafoola said. "Does anyone have any last questions for Sparky?"

"I have something to say," Billy said, raising both his hands at once. "We still have no proof at all that Sparky's story is somewhat true."

"When was the last time anyone ever saw a real pirate walking down the street?" Bucky asked. "I'll tell you—never."

"We believe in dinosaurs even though we didn't see them," Jill said.

"That's a good point," Tony said.

"Once again, it's not a good point," Billy said. "We believe in dinosaurs because we've found their bones."

My fourth-grade English class broke out into a loud chatter. Some kids believed I was a pirate captain, and some kids didn't believe I was a pirate captain.

"Sparky, it looks like the English class has run aground," Mrs. Chatafoola said. "If you want, you can take your seat."

I raised my cane and stood strong and tall. "I'm a pirate captain!"

A hush fell over the class as kids leaned forward in their seats. They were waiting for me to show proof that I was indeed a pirate captain and how my story was somewhat true.

"Well get on with it," Bucky said.

"I have a million other things I could be doing right now," Billy said.

"No, you don't," Jill said. "The only two things kids have to think about doing are making mud pies and watching cartoons."

"Sparky, tell us about this proof," Leo said.

The north wind twirled up from my toes all the way up to my nose. "I can tell you something. I hope something will be enough. It was enough for me. My adventure started with three pirates who sailed the waters of a wishing well. Upon the greatest of all lucky charms, I placed my hope of being a pirate captain."

"So that's the something you wanted to tell us?" Bucky asked. "You want us to believe in wishing wells?"

"You're trying to tell us your turtle's noodle is the greatest of all lucky charms?" Billy asked.

"Yes, and yes again," I said.

"Sparky, is that your proof?" Leo asked.

"One last thing," I said. "Those three pirates made me sad, made me happy, they made me cry and made me laugh. What's more real than that?"

"Ooooooooooh! Sparky's story is somewhat true," all the kids in my class said.

Well... except for Billy and Bucky who just said, "Booooooo!"

Chapter 14

30 years later. Where are they now?

Bucky grew up to become a dentist. His favorite thing to do is drill for cavities in children's teeth.

Billy has spent every day for the last 30 years traveling to faraway lands, trying to prove pirates and unicorns aren't for real, but so far has failed to do so.

Leo grew up to be a judge and is a fine one at that.

Jill went on to be one of the greatest self-help speakers in the country.

Tony became a scientist and discovered that turtles are smarter than humans.

Sparky grew up... I take that back. Sparky never grew up and spends her time writing fun stories that kids love to read.

The End

About the author

T. E. Antonino is an author of multiple genres for both adults and children. The author is currently working on two children's books that will be coming out soon!!

Follow T. E. Antonino on goodreads.com

Please post a review of this book online and let the world know how much your little one liked this book!

Made in the USA
Monee, IL
16 November 2023